Abraham Abulafia

Abraham Abulafia English Translations

Abraham Abulafia

Abraham Abulafia English Translations

ISBN/EAN: 9783741179624

Manufactured in Europe, USA, Canada, Australia, Japa

Cover: Foto ©Andreas Hilbeck / pixelio.de

Manufactured and distributed by brebook publishing software
(www.brebook.com)

Abraham Abulafia

Abraham Abulafia English Translations

Get Ha-Shemot – Divorce of the Names

Open my eyes (עֵינַי גַּל, *Gal Einai*), that I may see wonderful things in your *Torah*. More precious to me (טוּב לִי, *Tov Li*) is the *Torah* from your mouth than thousands of pieces of silver and gold. [The initials of these two *Psukim* spell *Get*.]

Said the Author: Because the opinions of men vary extensively concerning the truth about perceptual and intellectual reality, and because of the ignorance that is essential to human nature, external and intermediate, and because of the errors of thought about words of prophesy, hidden and revealed, which testify to all and that awaken the sleepers in the dirt, dwellers of matter that are founded on dust (Job, 4:19).

The Lord has awakened me to inquire and clarify their roots and principles that are known to every *Maskil* (משכיל, intellectual person) from the letter compositions and names that are found in them. For these principles are much required and are highly beneficial to every person of reason in getting to the truth of these matters, and they perfect the *Nefesh* (נפש, here used as Mind or Psyche) of Man through the knowledge of the Awe of God. And Him I beseech to fulfill my purpose and request to teach and guide me on the nearest and straightest path to my purpose, which is in truth for the glory of His Blessed Name. For I am aware of reasons in myself that bar me from this investigation, and I should not have held it. And I saw, in truth, that the biggest barrier is my lack of knowledge of the true wisdom and the weakness of my intellect in divine matters, which are the true *Kabbalah*. And I observed other barriers that are physical; and therefore. [it is] not mentioned in the books of truth that they can prevent their owners from composing living and beneficial words of God [i.e. on divine matters]. So alone, I weighed in my mind the strongest barrier against the motivation that brings me to compose a book about the principles of truth and found that the benefit of such a work outweighs any reason why the truth is not accessible to me. And that is because the ignorance that bars me is not dependent on my will, while the benefit of the book outweighs it inasmuch as it is derived from my will. And I decided to inform every *Maskil* about my intellectual shortcomings, about the depth of my duty to compose these matters, and to make only general notes about them. For the details are too great for me and beyond my reach. And if some details are mentioned due to the looseness of my tongue wanting to explain something as far as my limited knowledge goes – and only as much as necessary to explain some principle or the matter at hand – let not the *Maskil* blame me for it; for these principles are great in themselves and my knowledge of them is little. However, if I mention something of the roots of true *Kabbalah*, I will only indicate it as something that must remain concealed – for I will not be a teller of secrets. Let he who can hear, hear, and he who fails, fail. I will begin the discussion with perceptual reality.

And the first principle I will state is that, from the sphere of the Zodiac to the Earth, there are 12 concentric spheres including the body of the Earth, and there is no void between them that does not contain any physical object at all. And above them all is a single sphere that surrounds everything within itself and motivates everything with its motion. And these 12 spheres contained in the first one are called perceptual reality, for they are physical. Everything physical is perceivable, even though there are in reality three spheres not perceived by the eye. And these are the uppermost one and the upper two elements down here: fire and wind. They are called perceptual because it was deduced that they are necessarily physical. And even the other spheres in heaven are invisible to the eye, if not by way of their planets and stars. For the fact that they seem blue to our eyes is due to the colors of the air, and the spheres themselves are highly transparent and invisible.

And further, along with the perceptual, there are qualities (ענײנים, *Inyanim*, lit. subject matters) superior to it by degree, and these are all the intellectual qualities. Truly, Man contains both perceptual and intellectual qualities, for small Man is created in the image of the whole world. Hence, he is also called the micro-world, while the whole of reality is called the macro-world and macro-anthropos [man]; and Man is called the micro-world, and micro-anthropos. The perceptual quality in Man is the body in general, and the intellectual quality is the *Nefesh* and its faculties, even though perception is one of them. And just as the truth about the intellectual qualities that accompany everything physical is concealed from most people, and as the perceptual and intellectual in the micro-world and the macro-world are revealed and concealed [respectively], so too in the words of prophesy there are many great concealed and revealed matters. The revealed ones are beneficial to all, while the concealed are beneficial only to the few who are the remnants to whom God beckons. And when someone conceives the secrets of *Torah*, he can conceive through them the reality of the intellectual qualities in God, and the separate intellects and intelligibles that are in His world, which are their [the perceptual] *Nefashot* and forces.

And know that the world is divided in three parts. The first part, which contains everything and is therefore called the intellectual substance, includes the intellect, the conceiver and the conceived. The intermediate part includes only the conceiver and the conceived in its essence; for it is not intellectual as the first — lacking in one degree, which is the most important — and that is because it has matter and form. The lowest part is merely conceived, lacking in two degrees that are the intellect and the conceiver, and that is also because it is composed of matter and form. Still, its degree is extremely base and coarse compared to the second degree. And indeed, only mankind, when its intellect [or intellectual faculty] is actualized in this base world, returns to the form of the superior world, an intellect, a conceiver and a conceived like its maker. "**So God created man in his own image**" (Genesis 1:27), and the essence of the Blessed Creator is the conception of all existence, which is why He is called intellect. However, His degree is far superior to any intellectual substance, and because He conceives Himself, He is also a conceiver; and He is called conceived because anyone who conceives himself with his intellect is conceived, and the conceiver and conceived are never different as long as the intellect is actualized, though if it is only potential, they are different. And the Blessed Creator does not potentially conceive but always actually. And this is a considerable thing to understand for anyone who does not understand the qualities of the intellect from his own essence. And thus, the Blessed Creator is called intellect, conceiver, and conceived. And when you know His secret, you shall know all the superior and inferior beings according to the intellect and the *Kabbalah*.

And know also that this applies generally to all actual conceivers, and there are no conceivers in the world. But the created beings are intellectual substances or conceiver substances that do not always actually conceive, with the exception of Man, who is a conceiver in substance at the origin of his being. Nevertheless, do not imagine that the actualized conceiving substances are on the same level as God, Who also possesses this quality as we have seen, for He alone is necessary, and everything without Him is merely possible. Therefore, they cannot resemble Him or share any quality with Him except by equivocation. And when Man's intellect is actualized, even though he is the lower *Merkava* (מרכבה, chariot, composition), he is also an intellectual substance, an intellect, a conceiver, and a conceived. And know that this is a considerable and hidden notion among the wise, and I have no intention to clarify this notion, for it is entirely known to the Knowers who found *Chen* (חן, grace, also an acronym for חַכְמַת הַנִסְתָּר, the hidden wisdom or *Kabbalah*) in the eyes of God and men. And I believe that when I mention bits of these and other kabbalistic notions that agree with the intellect, they will be greatly approved by knowledgeable people. But if they do not agree, I know well that those who are wise in their own eyes will approve nothing of them, unless they were kabbalists (מקובל, *Mekubal*), who will surely rejoice in them. And anyone who is to be called a complete kabbalist must know, at the very least, the five things that are mentioned in *Sefer Yetzira* – which is attributed to Abraham, who received it from Shem and Ever – and know that it is sublime.

And the five mentioned processes are generally called *Tzeiruf* (צירוף, combination) of the letters. And they are *Chakika* (חקיקה, engraving or legislating), *Chatziva* (חציבה, carving), *Shikul* (שיקול, weighing), *Hamira* (המירה, substitution, more commonly spelled *Hamara*,

המרה, or *Temurah*, תמורה), *Tzeiruf.* For that is how they are mentioned in *Sefer Yetzira*: "*Chakekan, Chatzvan, Shaklan, Hemiran, Tzeirfan*". And that is their general interpretation. *Chakika* relates to writing (ספרות, *Sifrut*, or maybe *Sfarot*, numerals?) for the writer (*Sofer*, סופר, also the sages who finalized the written form of the *Torah*) is called legislator. *Chatziva*, is ṭhe *Tikun* (תיקון, restitution or completion) of the letters and their separation to the point that each of them can be distinguished and their qualities understood. *Shikul* is their preparation and self-weighing, and *Gematrias* (גימטראות, numerical equations) and *Cheshbonot* (חשבונות, computations) are also included here. *Hamira* is the substitution of one letter with another, its *Temura* and exchange with another, as the letters אחה"ע and the like, and every letter has a *Temura*. And it is a glorious wisdom always to perform this as required – not to add or to subtract too much. *Tzeiruf* of the letters combines one letter with another without performing a *Hamira* at all, such as מא"ד דא"א דמ"א אמ"ד אד"מ מד"א. And this too is a glorious wisdom. And these are the means revealing the secrets of *Torah* and no others; and when the *Maskil* receives this great secret of these five processes, I know that he will greatly approve of all the secrets of *Kabbalah* that are known from the names that are equivocal, doubtful, metaphorical, conventional, synonymous, and the names that are unique to God due to His effects [actions]; and even from the name that is most glorious, awesome, unified, and *Meforash* (מפורש, literal), which is superior to all the names, and refers to the unification absolutely and without any equivocation. And it is known that the world is called by an equivocal name that refers to three distinct things; and it is a divine name that contains a name of the Blesses Creator, the names of angels, and even the names of the lower driving forces on earth. And because it was equivocal, the created beings could not persist until it was combined with a name that has no reference to anything in the world, and rather refers only to the Unified Substance without any *Harkava* (הרכבה, complexity) in anything. And yet it is a great secret of there being at that stage letters indicating the *Merkava*. And it is divided into two names: one to one, and one on one. And this is not due to *Shemot Ha'Etzem* (שמות העצם, proper or substantial names), heaven forbid, but is to indicate His mastery over creation, in the image of the *Merkava* that is divided in two – perceptual and intellectual – as we have said. And it refers to the two worlds: this world and the next; and a single one rides over them and rules the above and below. And that is the name that is unified in two letters, unified in three letters, and unified in four letters; and know it well:

[*Y* (י)] *Y"H* (י"ה) *YH"V* (יה"ו) *YHV"H* (יהו"ה), which is a single complete name. And by this name you will understand what is in front of you: *Yu"d* (יו"ד) *H"a* (ה"א) *V"v* (ו"ו) *H"a* (ה"א). And since their letters are nine, the end of the '*Cheshbon*' (חשבון, computation), you can now understand the secret [=] 'in which *Ha-Shem* – the Name – lives', if you are [one] of the true masters of *Kabbalah*, and do not turn to the sect of "the proud, and those who turn aside to false‧ gods" (Psalms 40:5). For these are superior secrets, and one should not study them except for their headlines and with people who are knowledgeable and God-fearing: "God confides in those who fear him; he makes his covenant known to them" (Psalms 25:14). And when you hear something about some names, and you know not what their qualities are, keep away from them until you understand their qualities or have heard them from a kabbalist. But a kabbalist will never give you the qualities other than in brief; and to benefit from them, mention them only for the sake of sanctifying God. And let not the words of God lay in your mouth except for the benefit of your heart; and your actions will draw you closer to God and will not keep you away if you want to follow His paths.

Now I return to the previous issue, and mention the kinds of equivocal names mentioned by Rabbi Shmuel Ibn Tibun in his interpretation of the foreign expressions in the *Guide to the Perplexed*, and he said that an **equivocal name** is when you find one word used as a name for different kinds, and one kind is not prior to the others in any way. For example the word *Ayin* (עין) could equally mean an eye or a fountain of water. And if I am brief about it, know that this is the issue with it. And he said further that a **metaphorical name** is when one [kind] is rightfully primary to the others, and the others resemble it in some detail like head and leg, which refer to organs of animals first, and then as a metaphor to the head of the bed and its leg. And he believes that the principle metaphors originate from names that refer primarily to mankind, to animals, to plants, or to inanimate objects, and priority should be given in that order; and then you can use it metaphorically according to your fancy. And he said that the matter of *Hashgacha* (השגחה, providence, watching over) is used metaphorically for God; it cannot refer to it directly, for it is inconceivable apart form Him; and therefore, the word *Hashgacha* refers primarily to the *Hashgacha* of mankind, and as a metaphor for divine *Hashgacha*. And the metaphorical names in this language are many, like bread, which is the food of the body in nature, but used as a metaphor for the food of the *Nefesh* – even as it lives –

and it is the wisdom and the *Torah* and many more like this. A **doubtful name**: the Rav in "*The Guide*" said that this is a name that will be used on the basis of a doubtful resemblance between one kind of thing and another, and this resemblance is only something accidental and does not make them of a single substance. And R. Shmuel Ibn Tibon said he believes these are actually equivocal names, and their equivocation is on the doubtful side — meaning the name is used primarily for one thing. And someone who uses it for something else takes these two things to be of the same kind — like the word 'image' used for the outline of a man perceived by the senses — and doubtfully for an imaginary outline. And the Rav [i.e. Rambam] mentioned that this is a doubtful name even when referring to the Blessed Creator, as in "and he sees the image of God" (Numbers, 12:8). And he [Ibn Tibun] thinks that this name is metaphorical. A **conventional name** is when the name is equivalent to a definition. And examples are many, as the definition of Man that is a speaking life form, and that can be said equally of Reuven, Shimon, Levi and Yehuda. And so, the definition of life form applies equally to plants and to sentient beings, to every living thing [i.e. a conventional name is the name of a universal]. A **synonymous name**: as the author of *Ha-Melamed* said, this is the opposite of the equivocal name for which there is no single definition, but the name itself remains the same, as in the name *Ayin*. Instead, in the synonym the definition remains the same, while the name changes like the names *Yayin* (יין) and *Chomer* (חמר, from the Aramaic חמרא) of which both mean wine. And after I discuss these names according to different interpreters, I will mention the other names and notions sufficiently for you to see the truth of my statements.

And I will state initially that the *Maskil* should only believe in these three: the perceived, the conceived, and the received (מקובל). For common sense is included in them, and thus does not require a separate definition. These three suffice, and that is their interpretation. The **perceived** is something that is known through the five senses, which are sight, hearing, smell, taste, and touch. The **conceived** is something that the intellect accepts and knows once it is demonstrated to it – such as arithmetics, the periods of the year, and *Gematrias*. And the **received** is something on which it is said 'such-and-such I have received from so-and-so'. And it is known that the perceived requires no proof, for a man will not ask when he sees light for proof that it is light. And so too for the primary conceptions such as that two is greater than one: there is no need for proof. And similarly, the received requires no proof, for it is sufficient for the receiver to say 'so I have received'. But all the other conceptions are not to be accepted unless proven, either by a perception that is as evident as a proof or by an argument of reason. But everything we said about proof concerns conceptions alone. And when a man believes in these three things, he can rightfully claim to believe and say I believe such-and-such from the *Kabbalah* [or by receiving]. And no one will ever disagree with him unless they will not admit truth, and these are a negligible minority.

Next, I state that my sole intention in this book is to point out to the masters of the names the errors that they possess and warn them not to believe them until they know what supports them and to verify their belief in the true names that awaken every sleeper. And if I am successful with them I will give thanks to God, but if not I will thank God for helping me to write the truth and to remove all falsehood from this book of mine that is chosen for the glory of God.

And because I remove the false names that lack true wisdom, I called this work "**Divorce of the Names**", whose significance comes from the two *Psukim* that I quote at the head of this work: *Gal Einai* and *Tov Li*. And I have another great secret in this name of *Gimel* ('ג) and *Tet* ('ט), which you will hear below, God willing. And this is also the secret of the divorce paper written by the husband to his wife containing 12 lines – no more, no less – to remove her from him. Furthermore, [it points to] one of the superior names on which it is said "that [*Zeh*, זה, and ז"ה = 12 in *Gematria*] is My Name forever" (Exodus 3:15), "that (*Zeh*) is my god" (Exodus 15:2), etc.; and I exchanged one (*Zeh*) with the other (*Zeh*), for they also number 12.

And I state that if a *Maskil* possesses names that he does not know the qualities of, let him not destroy them but keep them. For they might possess some qualities he is not aware of, and he will learn about later. And this comment against destroying a name among names stems from my belief that if you destroy a holy name, you are punished. And therefore, it is good to grasp the one and not let go of the other (Ecclesiastes 7:18). For I only warned you against believing them without the wisdom and the benefit of knowing the truth about them. And all I am awakening you to is in order that you do not waste your days chasing figments and things of no value; rather chase always after the truth, and you shall find it. And it [or He] will always be with you and you with it [or Him]. And do not think about the issue of true names and secrets, when your aim is to achieve the highest degree of the perceptual reality with their help, to perfect the body for its benefit – as the gullible do. Therefore, chase after knowledge and do not seek the names for the sake of truth because it is truth, but vice versa. It is wrong to do so, and that is not the path of the *Maskilim*. Rather, seek the truth always because of the importance of finding [your own] essence. Indeed, the reasons that put a stop to knowledge for most people is that they seek things that their existence is not depended upon and because they think that anyone who knows those things will die prematurely, or go crazy, or that at least something bad will happen to him. And they do not understand that Man lives by the knowledge of truth and will die when removed from it. And everyone is obliged by *Torah* and by reason to seek the truth and accept it even from books, for truth is not distinguished according to who said it but by its own marks. And so, truth is what must essentially be believed. And do not blame me if at times I use the word truth and its relatives in the masculine and at other times in the feminine, for I will not be grammatical about it but use it as befits the situation, as with any word that can be understood both ways. And I cannot write the names applicable to the perceptual and the intellectual for you until I describe the form of the world at large; and then, I will demonstrate to you all that is contained therein. And the names for all these things that are the primary kinds and some of their details can only be known by means of prophesy, which has been taken away from us by our sins. And what we have left is just a small sample, some of which we have received from a teacher. And some of it is recorded in the Written *Torah*, some of it in the Oral *Torah*, and some in the recent books of *Kabbalah* lately written; and some [of it is] in the books of the philosophers. And with the help of God, and when possible, we have collected them together to benefit from them in few words, on broad issues. For it was our intention to benefit the reader by letting him grasp some of the names wherein wisdom is embedded. And so, in order to perfect the

Nefesh of man and guide it on the right path, we must mention first the whole of existence and its qualities – for the truth about everything may be derived from that. This is our way of loving and fearing Him, because of the benefit to our *Nefesh* and our body. And we should love Him because of His supremacy in all His effects [actions], but we should fear Him because of His *Midot* [מידות, attributes]. For it is known that there cannot be a lover who never saw his beloved, if his love is to be complete and not be dependent on anything. And there you have the form that the people of science discovered for all existence with absolute proofs. And because they wrote extensively about their proofs, I need not write them but only mention it as it is drawn in the intellect and outside it, in hard facts. And I will also inform you of what *Kabbalah* says about it in a different matter. And I will draw out for you all of the spheres – one after the other – until you are able to speak easily about them, and in an instant draw them into your heart, for this has many benefits – as the scientists explained – for knowing how all the parts hang together. And I will draw it out for you:

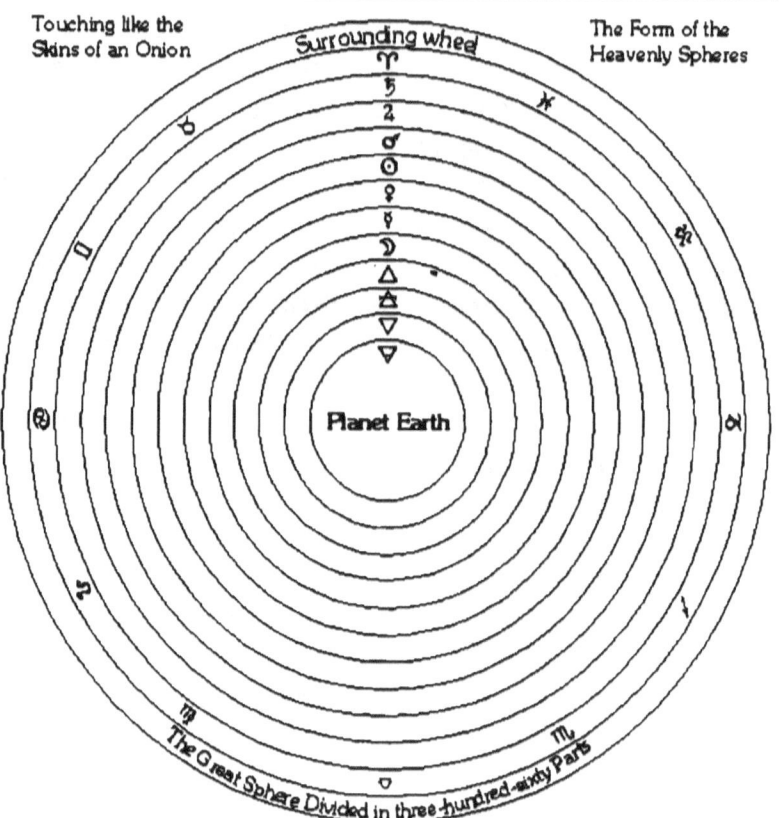

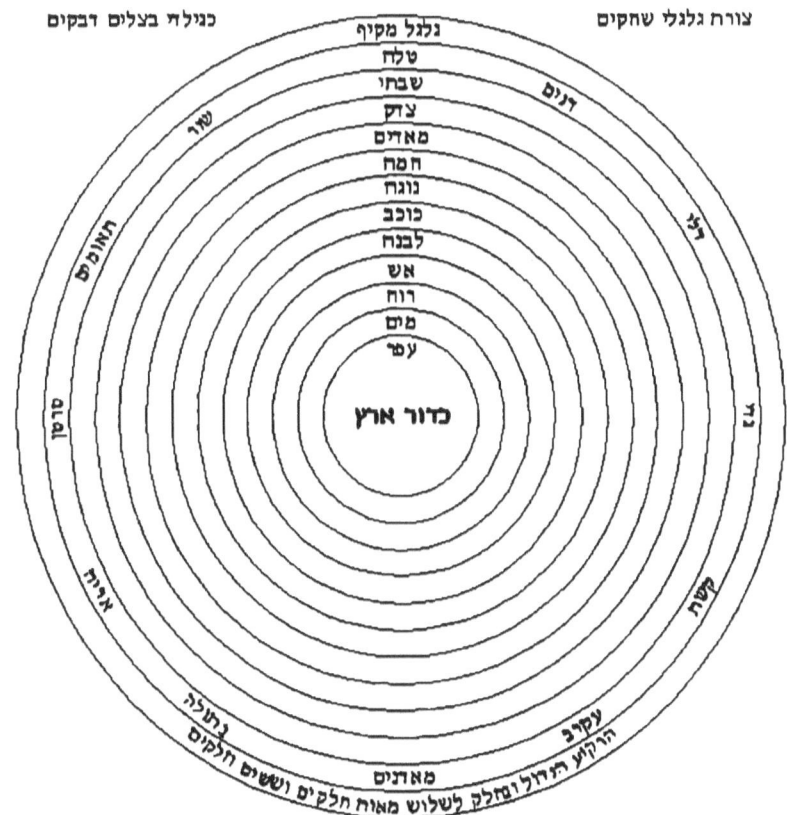

And this is the interpretation of this form as a whole, which is of spheres surrounding and being surrounded in this circular form — the physical world bound as one. And there are two types of matter in the two worlds: the superior and inferior, in the forms of head and legs. For so it is said, "**Heaven is my throne, and the earth is my footstool**" (Isaiah 66:1), and none is as fine as the uppermost among them, which is the simplest among them. Yet, it also is matter and form, and it surrounds everything and sets everything in motion. And it is called *Rakia* (רקיע, firmament) and *Aravot* (ערבות, lit. willows).

There is no physical body beyond it, and it contains no planet or constellation. *Sefer Yetzira* says of this sphere, "the sphere in the year is like a king in his state", for it rules. And if it moves, it is evidently not divine, for the divine is above it and does not move but sets everything in motion; for it is proven that He is neither physical body nor force. And we will discuss this further below, with God's help, for this is not the proper place for it. And the bodies of all the spheres stand inside this circumspective sphere, but it is the first when we compare it to what is inside it, and we use the scale of top to bottom. And if we use the inverse scale from bottom to top, and we state what we know about it [then we shall do] as Jacob our Partiarch did, whose share is in it. Though we find that Ezekiel mentions it from top to bottom, there is no harm in that, for each seer states it as it is shown to him, whether in a vision or in a dream.

And I will state that the Earth is solid as a solid sphere, and its true essence and substance is earth alone; although we know that in fact it is composed of the four elements, we must only interpret it according to its essential form. And the water surrounds both hemispheres according to one opinion and one hemisphere according to another, and one hemisphere is exposed without water – the one that is required for [land] life. And the other part that was supposed to be water is turned into air, which is finer than water. And that rises up to a place where the water becomes water again, though it was always elementally water, and they spill down from there. And this is as high as the vapor (אד) will rise, as it is written **"And vapor came up from the earth and watered the whole surface of the ground"** (Genesis, 2:6). Up to the surface of the earth, and beyond that, air surrounds water. And there is something that we should mention here after what we just said.

However, it is worthy of being concealed, and the headlines we mentioned above are enough; and we will trust in those who know it fully. And fire surrounds air on all sides, and these are called the four elements, which are one [kind of] matter. And from then onwards, the sphere of the moon surrounds the sphere of fire; and the sphere of Mercury [surrounds] the sphere of the moon; and the sphere of Venus surrounds the sphere of Mercury; and the sphere of the sun surrounds the sphere of Venus; and the sphere of Mars surrounds the sphere of the sun; and the sphere of Jupiter surrounds the sphere of Mars; and the sphere of Saturn surrounds the sphere of Jupiter. And these are the seven spheres, and the seven planets we mentioned are their planets. And above them is the sphere of the fixed stars in which there are twelve signs, and it surrounds the sphere of Saturn. And above all is the uppermost sphere, which surrounds the spheres of the signs. And it is the first among them – as we said – from the perspective of the superior ones, but is the last one for us who live at the bottom, dwellers in the dust.

And now I will point out to you how the whole world, as mentioned according to this drawing, is *Echad* (אחד, one), for the circumspective sphere is unique, because it contains nothing but the forces that flow down from it. But other, real physical bodies, it does not contain at all, and it is unique among all spheres. And it is referred to by the letter *Aleph* ('א = 1 in *Gematria*) of *Echad*. And below it are the eight spheres that have heavenly bodies in them, indicated by the letter Chet ('ח = 8 in *Gematria*) of *Echad*. Below them are the four elements of fire, air, water, and earth, each surrounding the Earth, for the Earth is surrounded but not surrounding, ridden but it does not ride, like the point in the middle of a circle. And the letter *Dalet* ('ד = 4 in

Gematria) of *Echad* indicates these elements. And so, you can get to know by reason and by the way of *Kabbalah* that the whole world is *Echad*. And since it is *Echad*, it is ruled by the *Echad*, blessed be He. And therefore, the number of the spheres is 13, the sum of [the word] *Echad*. Keep this secret and know it, for it is sublime, conceived, and received, and it is the Unified Name in general.

Side note [in the original manuscript, probably by the copyist]: I found more on the structure of the world and the courses of the year in a different manuscript, and I included these elucidations here, though they do not belong to the *Get*. And this is the content of the elucidation:

Know today that your God is not contained in space, and is by definition beyond [the categories of] space or time or investigation. (For) He is *Echad* beyond all comprehension, and no investigation is possible in Him, and He does not possess a body that is composed of parts. And He is the Cause for all causes, and He is *Echad* and unified as His name is unified, and brings about great, famous wonders that no one can deny. And this name is divided in *Echad*, and it is *Echad*, and even when it is divided, the parts sum up to *Echad*, for the name of 4 letters sums up to 26; and when you divide it, each part is 13, which is the sum of [the word] *Echad*. And nothing is missing, for it is impossible for it to contain too much or too little, or change from what it is; for He is unified in His *Midot*, even though He has many different names and *Midot*. He is unified in all of them, and they are unified in Him. And He is the beginning of the beginning, for the beginning of *Cheshbon* (חשבון, computation) is *Echad*, which is His name that is mentioned in all things. And there is no primordial beginning, for everything was created out of nothing. Concerning the end of research, if someone were to investigate His effects [actions], the investigation will terminate at the beginning of the first effect, at the point where everything that exists in this lower world has a cause above, from which it is derived, in the foundation of the beginning: the 32 paths of wisdom, the creation and existence of everything in an intellectual fashion, not in a physical body but purely intellectually. Watching it is only possible in *Ratzo Vashov* (רצוא ושוב, reaching back and forth), meaning when they rise to receive *Shefa* (שפע, affluence) from above, they immediately recede a little, reaching backwards, and then returning to rise and reach forwards a little, and continuing to move in this fashion until they receive *Shefa Berachot* (ברכות, blessings). "**The** ***Chayot* sped back and forth like flashes of lightning**" (Ezekiel 1:14). The meaning of lightning (בזק) here is that they acquire an image according to their effects, and when they operate, they acquire forms that are adequate for the effects they have, whether for good or evil. And this form is invisible to human eyes except for those with a pure *Nefesh*, such as the *Chassidim* (חסידים, ascetics) and the sons of prophets. And horses of fire are the intellect's own forms, as it is written "**and horses of fire**" (II Kings 2:11), sometimes for *Din* (דין, judgment), sometimes for *Rachamim* (רחמים, mercy, compassion), like spirits; for they sometimes become spirits when they run errands. "And the voice of thin silence" (I kings, 19:12), meaning they are non-perceptual, and he creates angels of *Rachamim* at times of will, but at times of wrath he creates angels of *Din*. And He gave *Hod* (הוד, splendor, magnificence) to *Vilon* (וילון, lit. curtain, also a name for the firmament). These are the seven intellectual spheres – one above the other – in which two different sections were sanctified to effect inferior beings, each according to its fashion. And He produced something out of nothing, and nothing into something He made; and from the absolutely possible He created *Tohu* (תהו, primordial chaos), which is the primal state of matter known as formless matter. And this *Tohu* is the origin of the two kinds of matter: that of the heavens, which is simple, and that of the earth, which is compound. And as I said, the superior one is simple and the abode of the planets, while the inferior is complex, and it revolves below in the four spheres of fire, air, water, and earth. And He constructed a circle around the spheres [of the elements] like sheets, and these are the seven planets that shine on the world. And they persist without change, and their spheres persist without any accidents occurring in them until everything returns to its original substance, as it is written, **"for the heavens shall vanish away like smoke"** (Isaiah 51:6), at the end of the six thousand years.

…They are…spheres within spheres, for this is the character of the world of the spheres and of the elements. And they are made one inside the other: the spheres are one within the other as the skins of an onion, and they are one within the other. And they are hollow, and the radius of the sphere emerges from the Earth, which is solid. The ninth sphere is called the circumspective sphere; it surrounds everything and revolves from east to west. And its east to west course cancels the movement of the other spheres, which revolve from west to east; so, they also revolve from east to west like the ninth that drives them. And within it He has engraved (חקק, *Chakak*) the eighth one, which is the sphere of the 12 signs that are fixed on it; and these are the 12 signs in four quarters. For the signs are divided into quarters: 3 having the force of air, 3 having the force of water, 3 having the force of earth, and 3 having the force of fire. And they are the sources of cold, heat, dryness, and moisture. And the sphere of the zodiac is fixed on two hinges: at the southern and northern tips. And all the stars revolve in this eighth sphere beyond the spheres of the planets – one planet to one sphere – and they are means for effecting [operating] on the world, while the zodiac is for the months. And these 7 planets are responsible for the fetus developing in its mother's womb, each operating during one first day of the month. And in seven months the fetus acquires all its functions; and therefore, its form is complete in 7 months, and if it is born it survives. And the last two that are Jupiter and Saturn are then repeated. And if it is born in the ninth month, then the baby lives. But if it is born in the eight month in which the force of Saturn is active, it will die nevertheless, and it is called an eighth born, which is a stillborn. And those 7 planets have authority over the whole of the inferior world, and the planet that appears at the break of day or the break of night is mostly active during that time. And He has carved (חצב, *Chatzav*) light, meaning that He wanted the spheres to contain a shining object to shed light on the world. And He put up lamps; He put the two lamps up in the spheres: one to shine during the day and one during the night.

The sun revolves around the zodiac in a year, which is 360 degrees, a little less than one degree per day, and it travels 13 degrees per day. When they shine, it is their purpose to shine, and sometimes they contain their light in a single ray as at the beginnings of months, or during eclipses, or in other cases. And they create the order of the seasons, the growth of trees and grasses, and the ripening of fruits. They also cause many wonders and miracles, as it is written, "[and they became signs] (I will show wonders) in the heavens and on the earth, blood and fire and billows of smoke" (Joel 3:3); sawing and reaping, as it is written, "**seedtime and harvest, cold and heat, summer and winter**" (Genesis 8:22), and the measure of day and night, as it is written, "**and for the days**" (Genesis 1:14); and the end of years of the seasons "**and for the years**" (Ibid.), meaning that the year of the six days is complete. And the year of the moon is close to 30 days. And the seasons are 4: when the sun enters the sign of Aries, the sign of Cancer, the sign of Libra, and the sign of Capricorn. "**And for the births**" (Ibid.), which are the births of the moon. And *Chazal* said: "The moon is not renewed in less than 29 days and a half, and two thirds of an hour and 72 parts" (Tract *Rosh HaShana*, 25). And at the end of every 19 years the cycles of the sun and the moon meet. And of the doors of the abyss, it is said, "**Let the water under the sky be gathered**" (Genesis 1:9), and they stood in the abyss, as it is written, "**a channel for the torrents of rain**" (Job 38:25). And the knot of the foundation of *Din* is the formless matter of the Earth, which is below the spheres, from which the 4 spheres upon which the world stands are made; and these are the spheres of the elements, which form cold, heat, dryness, and moisture. He wielded the 4 separate spheres together, and they mixed together until each sphere was changed by the impact of the others. Among them, 2 are heavy and descend: water and earth; and 2 are light, and these are fire and wind; and they ascend due to their lightness and fineness. And I did not find more on this issue. In a different place I found more on this topic, and it is from the introduction of the interpretation of the *Torah* by R. Tzedaka Halevi of the town of Gaza; and that too was an elucidation not from the body of the text (here ends the side note).

God created three worlds: the superior world, the intermediate world, and the inferior world. The description of creation specifically mentions only two, while the superior world is only indicated and not clarified, just as the world to come is not clarified but indicated, for it is not required; and it is a deep and sublime secret. And *Chazal* [our sages of blessed memory] said that the angels were created on the second day, but on the first day nothing was created save for the primal matter and the concealed light, for He was *Echad* and His name was *Echad*; all these issues are too deep to be discussed. And God created the two worlds together, as it is written, "**when I summon them, they all stand up together**" (Isaiah 48:13). And He created them out of void and nothingness, from *Tohu* to *Bohu* (בהו, found along with תהו in the description of the original chaos), and from *Bohu* to being. And he clothed each one with its proper existence, according to choice and will; and in [one of] them stand the sphere[s], whose members persist and act without change, loss, or destruction. As it is written, "**He set them in place for ever and ever**" (Psalms, 148:6). Their initial purpose is to act for the sake of God, and their second purpose is to effect the lower world, which is the world of generation and destruction. And their purpose is not for their own sake but for the sake of their creator; but they and their desires have effects according to their purpose, for they are effective. And the two worlds are bound together with a stable and persistent knot made with the force of their maker in *Gvura* (גבורה, here used as potency, power).

God created three worlds: the superior world, the intermediate world, and the inferior world. The description of creation specifically mentions only two, while the superior world is only indicated and not clarified, just as the world to come is not clarified but indicated, for it is not required; and it is a deep and sublime secret. And what *Chazal* [our sages of blessed memory] said is that the angels were created on the second day, but on the first day nothing was created by the primal matter and the concealed light, for He was *Echad* (One) and His Name was *Echad.* All these issues are too deep to be discussed. And God created the two worlds together, as it is written, **"when I summon them, they all stand up together"** (Isaiah 48:13). And He created them out of void and nothingness, from *Tohu* to *Bohu* (בהו, found along with תהו in the description of the original chaos), and from *Bohu* to being. And he clothed each one with its proper existence, according to choice and will, and in [one of] them stand the sphere[s], whose members persist and act without change, loss, or destruction. As it is written, **"He set them in place for ever and ever"** (Psalms, 148:6). Their primary purpose is to act for the sake of God, and their secondary purpose is to act on the lower world, which is the world of generation and destruction. And their purpose is not for their own sake, but for the sake of their creator; but they and their desires act according to their purpose, for they are active. And the two worlds are bound together with a stable and persistent knot made with the force of their maker in *Gvura* (גבורה, here used as potency, power).

And the inferior beings are effected [acted upon], and are generated and destroyed: generated as the elements combine, and destroyed as they separate. For they receive all these changes and re-compositions from the motion of the sphere, without rest and without ever either fully existing or becoming extinct, as the divine decrees. And their formless matter is a matter that receives the *Shefa* of the motion of the sphere. And as the latter never cease from their revolutions, so the former never cease from generation and destruction as the sphere revolves. And the 4 elements are made of very fine and invisible parts, and when they are mixed together they combine; and what should be generated by them is generated; and what should be destroyed is destroyed, by the aforementioned motion by the will of God. The bodies of the spheres are made of parts, but they are not compound. And they will not bear to be divided or separated. They are clear and translucent (ספירי), and in order to do the will of their maker, have received eternal life from the moment of their creation – existing forever. But motion can only happen in a physical body. And that body [of the spheres] has no movement, location, or boundaries, no beginning and no end. Circular motion has no beginning and no end; and therefore, it is intermediate between the physical and the non-physical. And motion causes the qualities of time, generation, and destruction.

And the motion of the ninth, which is *Aravot*, is the daily 24 hours, half day and half night, and it revolves from east to west. And according to the borders of the climates, the day exceeds the night or falls behind it by a little or by much. For in the first climate, it exceeds or falls behind very slightly and unnoticeably, and the day and night are equal throughout the year. And in the second climate, it exceeds or falls behind by an hour or so, depending on where you are [lit. and its beginning is different from its bulk]; and in the third climate two hours or more; and in the fourth climate up to 4 hours;- and in the fifth up to 5 hours; and the sixth up to six hours; and the seventh up to seven hours and more. All these are approximations, for the conditions at the beginning of a climate zone are not the same as at its end [lit. its beginning is different form its end]. And beyond these seven climates, no grass or animal can exist because of the extreme cold of winter and the extreme warmth of summer. And the sphere called *Aravot* is superior to all the other spheres; the elements are inside it, and it excels them.

This is why it has no stars or planets, and they all move with its motion, for they are subordinated to it due to its great excellence over them. And its physical magnitude is beyond human investigation; only its Maker Whose knowledge is beyond knowledge [surpasses it], for He created it with this magnitude; for it is the first among physical bodies, and the speed of its motion is due to the vastness of its desire. And all the spheres are driven along because of it, and it is the intermediary between the world of the angels and the physical body of the spheres, even though there is no physical space [lit. place, מקום] there, but only separate forms that no body can contain, the space of those who stand before Him, who are close to Him. And [then there is] the motion of the eight, which is below *Aravot*, and it is full of stars, for all the stars are fixed on it except the 7 planets, for each of them has its own sphere, as explained by the science of astronomy. And it revolves from west to east once every 24 thousand years, in the inverse direction to the motion of the upper daily one, as is the motion of all the rest of the spheres. And a year is for the motion of the sun, while a month is for the motion of the moon, as it is said, "**And they became signs**" (Genesis, 1:14), etc. And every change in the inferior world takes place according to the motion of the remaining five planets, of the generation, the destruction, the vapours, the clouds, and the rain. And they are the immediate cause of every change – those mentioned and the many changes in the world.

And the seven planets receive power and *Shefa* from the upper ones: the ninth and the eighth, which are the *Shmei Shamaim* (שמי שמים, the heavens of the heavens); and they have effects on the inferior ones due to their great excellence, such that the moon receives all of them, as it is below them all. And it transfers them to the world of the elements, the very essence of its effects being on the born, the seas, and rivers, as the wise have testified; and all these things to endless detail, for it is the neighbour of the upper elements, and its body is smooth, black, and devoid of any light. It receives it from the light of the sun; as the light touches it, it brightens up and shines. And below it is the element of fire; their boundaries touch, for there is no void between them. And the element of wind, which is the air, touches the element of fire. And those are the two translucent elements, close to the translucence of the heavens, but not of the same substance as the body of the heavens. And as the body of the heavens does not cover the light of the heavenly bodies, so those two elements do not cover their light or prevent them from being seen. And the fire is warm, fine, and pure; and the wind below it is humid and warm; and the light of the sun brings warmth to the other elements and heats them, and they react because they are so fine. And concerning every disturbance that you see in the air of the smokes and vapours, the moist ones come from rain, and the dry ones from smoke. And [among] the stars, the comets [or maybe meteors] are of that kind. He created known beings [הוא ברא בריות ידועים, or maybe: there are those who know that]; they are not stars, but of the smoke of the elements, and they shine in the element of fire. And when you see the sun during sunrise or sunset, and it is red or white, and you are able to look at it, this is because of the vapours that rise in the thick air. And now, we return to the body of the text.

And now my son, after we clarified the form of the perceptual world, we will talk briefly about the intellectual as far as we know. For Aristotle said he believed that the *Shefa* flows down from God, Who is the cause of everything, and it flows on a single separate intellect, which is the immediate effect of God. And I will state that it sets the circumspective sphere in motion, and from it flow eight more separate intellects; and each one sets one of the mentioned spheres in motion, down to the sphere of the moon. And there is a single intellect that motivates everything under the moon according to the philosophers, which they call the Active Intellect. And *Chazal* [our sages of blessed memory] called it *Ishim* (אישים, personalities, a type of angels), and so did the Rav interpret in the *Guide* [*To the Perplexed*]. And he writes that they are shining angels who speak to the prophets; and therefore, they are called *Ishim*. And we have deep and wonderful secrets in all that from the *Kabbalah*, and we will indicate them in brief as far as we can. And I already told every *Maskil* that everything that one is said to believe by *Kabbalah* requires no proof. For you only prove something that the intellect does not accept at first sight. And what has been received, while it also requires much careful contemplation, still, once you understand it, you cannot prove it; thus, we call it received; we discard the need for proof, as it is impossible. And if it is possible to prove it, we call it something conceived. And it is known that the conceived is superior to the received, for the conceived, once proven, is uncontroversial and can never be falsified, and the intellect must believe it. But we do not call this "belief", but rather "knowledge", for true knowledge is what makes it superior. And something received is [always] falsifiable, and it is possible to claim that this received thing is a mistake of your teacher of *Kabbalah*. And hence, a man does not truly know what he cannot prove. And therefore, we call received something that we believe because we have received it; and even though it cannot be proven, we are still left with belief instead of knowledge, such as the case of creation out of nothing, which is received among us, as mentioned above. And because it is impossible, [the philosophers] challenge us to bring a proof for the creation out of nothing, to contradict their error that the world is eternal and uncreated. And even we, who believe that the world is created, cannot prove beyond doubt that the world is created. Therefore, we are left with our belief [or faith] as if it is engraved in our hearts in place of the knowledge that it is created.

And this goes for any received issue, which falsifying goes against our true *Torah*. And so the received thing rises to the same level as the conceived, and it is even superior to it to some degree, which is that we have unique, received issues that the intellect alone could never conceive, unless by way of prophecy telling it so; and that is impossible, for there is no proof for it superior to any other proof. But because the human intellect is weak in nature, these issues were left to the stuff of stories and narrations, which we know will not tell lies. As it is said **"He Who is the Glory of Israel does not lie or change His mind; for He is not a man, that He should change His mind"** (I Samuel, 15:29). And the masses are told without proof that God is one. Even though, as it is known, there are many proofs of that fact, the mind of the masses is too weak to conceive them. Therefore, it was left as a matter of *Kabbalah*, which is sufficient for them. .

And similarly, *Kabbalah* from the mouth of prophesy to the prophet is also sufficient, and [also] to others who hear it from him or read it in his book. For books indicate the knowledge of their authors, and also testify to which school they belong among all the schools of authors, for they are divided in [the levels of] their knowledge. Some write out of prophesy, some out of *Ruach Ha-Kodesh* (רוח הקודש,

holy spirit), some out of faith, some merely out of thinking, and some out of their fancy. And the intentions behind the writing are also different. Some write for the benefit of the *Nefesh* and nothing else, and that intention is the noblest in its purpose of all the intentions. And there are those who aim for a physical benefit; and those who aim for power and honours; and those who intend to degrade the words of others out of the envy and hatred between them, in order to refine his colleagues and show his colleagues a reason why he is more of an intellectual than another author. And this is the very basest intention and a bad trait not to be found in those with a wholesome intellect. And if nature strives to force him to it, he should abstain with his intellect, weakly at first, until his intellect overcomes his nature, which is the *Yetzer Ha-Ra* (יצר הרע, evil impulse). However, if his intention is to correct the words of another, if they contain errors or something went unnoticed by the author because of the shortcomings of his intellect in the issues he was writing about, and all his intent is *Leshem Shamaim* (לשם שמים, lit. for the sake of heaven, an expression meaning 'to do what is right'), to remove error, and draw closer to the truth, and he demonstrates that mystery in his work, this is the way of respect among the *Maskilim*. And he indicates the places where there are errors in the texts they possess. And I claim that this is a great *Mitzva* to do, to save others from failing where he failed. And I apply the same measure to this, my own work as well. And may the author who corrects me be blessed, and God – praised be He – knows and is my witness, for He alone knows my intentions, that when I wrote above about the forgeries of the names, this was my intention. And I already apologised for it, and said that they must not be destroyed, for they might contain some matter [of truth] unknown to the author of this text, meaning those in possession of those [names], but not the author. And after mentioning the perceptual and intellectual in general, I will now write about the body and *Nefesh* in general, and then mention the names that apply to everything as I set out to do. And I will clarify them as much as I can for the *Maskil* who is a *Kabbalist* to understand their benefit to him, and what will give him pleasure with the help of God.

And I will state that all the different compositions are found also in Man, for he is the ultimate composition, being the last created. And he was created for the benefit of his *Nefesh*, which is the purpose intended for it, and so the body exists with it to help and to attend, like the wife is with her husband as a helper to him. As it is written, "I **will make a helper opposite to him**" (Genesis, 2:18), and *Chazal* interpreted it – if he is worthy [it is] a helper, if he is unworthy an opposition. And the body is composed initially of the four elements, and it gets its matter and form when it is a seed; and the body slowly changes from its initial existence, and takes the form of flora; and then of fauna, and eventually the speaking form; and then the form of the intellect. And it changes time after time until it emerges from potentiality to full realisation, which is the *Dveikut* (דביקות, adhesion) to the superior ones. And the 248 organs of the living body are all required by these forms to produce everything contained in them from potentiality to actuality. And it is known that all the deeds of mankind that follow the paths of God come by the power of the intellect that touches (*Davek*, דבק) the very essence of the *Nefesh*, while all that follow other paths, i.e. other than God, come from created nature, which deceives it [or him]. And this is the *Yetzer Ha-Ra*, and this is *Satan*, and this is the Angel of Death; and this is the Primordial Serpent. For you already know what *Chazal* said: 'when

the woman is created, the *Yetzer Ha-Ra* is created with it'
(*Bereshit Raba*, section 17, chapter 6), and you know the
secret of man and woman, as I mentioned it to you above.
And it exists in all his deeds, even though they follow from
nature; and there is no escaping them, or there is, but they
were intended in order to conceive the truth and do good
following God. For example, the mouth of a man is natural
to him as it is to other animals, and he necessarily requires
nourishment; if the intention behind his nourishment –
when he eats and drinks – is to have a healthy body and
benefit from this food so that he may worship his Creator
in health alone – not in order to taste sweet things, and
not just so that his body will be without illness –
undoubtedly, this [kind of] deed is also truly *Leshem
Shamaim*, for everything follows the intention, and the
heart leans towards mercy. Even if his deeds or words
contain things that should have been rejected, and they
come in place of what could benefit the intention
concerned, or as an overwhelming need, it means nothing.
For it is unworthy of the *Maskil* to examine any particular
deed unless by the utmost truthfulness, to find merit in it
wherever it could possibly be found.

And because I rely on the Rav in the *Guide*, and what he
said about it in his interpretation of *Avot*, I refrain from
expanding on this issue, for what he said is surely enough.
And if what he said about it is not enough, then it is
needless to state that anything I say about it will never be
enough, and so I rely on him. And I believe that it will not
escape the *Maskil* what he meant when he interpreted that
Masechta (מסכתא, a tract of *Mishna*) in ways that follow
the conclusions of the *Guide*. After having mentioned the
general makeup of Man with his body, *Nefesh*, and
activities, [and] to which of their sides he should be drawn
in order to achieve the purpose intended for his existence,

and for him to be found alive and among the living at the Resurrection of the Dead and live in *Olam Ha-Ba* (עולם הבא, the world to come), which is without end, I now proceed to mention all the names I intended that indicate the mysteries of the *Torah*, and that promotes the *Nefesh*'s efforts to believe the truth and to falsify the false that has no existence. For falsity is nothing but the lack of truth. However, truth always sustains the world and persists always in itself. And that is what *Chazal* meant when they said: "The world stands on three things: on *Din* (דין, Judgment), on truth, and on peace. As it is written, '**Render truth and a peaceful judgment in your courts**' (Zecharia 8:16)" (*Avot* 1:17).

And it is known that these three things are all dependent on truth, as it is written, "**Administer true judgment**" (Zecharia 7:9), and "**words of peace and truth**" (Esther 9:30). Meaning that the words of peace are true, and peace will forever exist together with truth when the truth is known on all its sides. However, if even a single side of all the sides of truth is missing, then truth will be absent and peace along with it, for it follows truth, and it is its cause and cannot be found without it. And do not be mislead by what *Chazal* said, that it is tolerable to lie for the sake of peace, for that lie you heard [them mentioning] is nothing but truth, from the aspect of its truth in the teller's heart. For if a person had understood that he was lied to in order to pacify his heart, then the teller would not have to lie; and therefore, it is not a lie but truth and peace self contained. And you will find the evidence that the world depends on truth in the alphabet, for its head, middle, and end are all truth [this relates to the first, middle and last letters – 'א, 'מ, 'ת, that together spell out the word אמת, *Emet*, truth]. And the rest of the letters depend on it, for all the letters correspond to reality and refer to it. And the remaining letters [besides these three] are in number like the number of attendants, and their sign is, "To *IHVH* your **God belong the heavens, even the heavens _ of the heavens**" (Deuteronomy 10:14). And that is apart from the *Kfulim* (כפולים, doubles, letters with an alternative spelling at the end of a word, [here referring specifically to the extra numerical value of this alternative spelling]), for the *Pshutim* (פשוטים, simple, the common form of the letters) are all in the sign of, "**fo"r trut"h (אמ"ת ה"ן = 496) you desire in the inner parts**" (Psalms 51:8) [the sum of all the letters of the alphabet in *Gematria* is 1495 = א. תצ"ה. When the 'א, signifying 1000, is counted as 1, this gives us תצ"ו = 496]. And with the *Kfulim*, the *Cheshbon* (חשבון, computation) of them all is *Shlemu"t* (שלמות, perfection = 776) [the *Kfulim* are ך, ם, ן, ף, ץ, with a total sum of 280. 496+280=776]. And in *Chesbon Aroch* (חשבון ארוך, a computation where the *Kfulim* ך, ם, ן, ף, ץ, are taken to represent 500, 600, 700, 800, 900 in *Gematria*) they sum up to 999 [the sum of all the *Kfulim* in *Gematria* is 3500 = ג. ת"ק. If the 'ג is counted as 3 we get תק"ג = 503. And 496+503=999]. And the 22 [basic] letters are equal to *Malchu"t* (מלכות, Kingship = 496). Now, if you take '*Shlemut* and extract *Emet* to one side [i.e subtract the value of אמ"ת = 441 from 776], you get [=] 'All the *Merkava* as *Echad* is truth' (כ"ל המרכב"ה אח"ד אמ"ת). And know that this in the secret of *Echad* explained above. And you will find that the *Cheshbon* of '*Malchut*, as you extract *Emet* to one side, is [=] 'everything is truth' (הכ"ל אמ"ת). And if you compute 999 and extract *Emet* to one side, you get [=] 'truth is primary to all' (ברא"ש הכ"ל אמ"ת). And that is the secret of everything real, for its reality is the truth on every side that has already been realized from the *Shefa* of truth, which is called by a name like the name of its lord. And he is *Metatron Sar Hapnim* (מטטרון שר הפנים, Metatron the master of the interior); and the letters testify that '*Sar Tzevaot* (שר צבאות, master of the hosts) [=] 'in the movement of the sphere' (בתנוע"ת הגלג"ל). And which sphere? The sphere that makes all of creation complete, which is the superior one that contains everything. And its motion testifies to its creator, for the *Cheshbon* repeats itself after 999; for one thousand (*Eleph*) returns to *Aleph* (א'), which is [numerically] one. And so the motion repeats itself in a circle at the end of every 999. And these are the nines, and similarly in all the letters there are three nines [ץ', צ', ט'], which are equal respectively to 9, 90, 900 in *Gematria*], in the image of the three worlds, and together they equal [9*3=] 27; and their secret [meaning] is *Kaf Zchut* (כף זכות, the scale of merit [*Zach*, ז"ך = 27]). And there are three *Merkavot* among the 22 letters, as in the entire intermediary image; and you will find that in their *Cheshbon* they testify to the truth, for they are vividly alive on every side; for the upper and simple *Merkava* is א"ב ג"ד, and if you remove the *Aleph* (א') that indicates *Emet*, you will be left with *Beged* (בג"ד, garment). And the middle *Merkava* is יכל"מ, and if you remove the *Mem* (מ') from it – which indicates the *Mem* of *Emet* – you are left with *K"li* (כל"י, vessel, instrument). And consequently with the bottom *Merkava*, which is קרש"ת; if you remove the *Tav* (ת') – which indicates the *Tav* of *Emet* – what is left is *Sheke"r* (שק"ר, falsehood, lie). And there you have it that once you remove truth, what remains is Garment [a common reference to the body], an Instrument of Falsehood, and truth remains on its own, self contained. And this is the beautiful secret, for it is the beginning of the paths of God, which are the paths of *Kabbalah*; and thus, I have drawn it out for you at the onset of my discussion.

And now I will inform you of another [name] that the whole world depends upon; and it is the beginning of every beginning and the end of all ends; and it is the *Shem Meforash* that is unified in all the paths of unification in the truth of its unification. And it also contains everything in all the paths of unification in the truth of its unification. And that is *YHVH* (יהוה), blessed be His name, Beshechmal"o (בשכמל"ו, acronym of the verse said after the *Shema*). And know that this blessed name contains all the names that are *Meforashim*, and they all follow from it. And it includes three books [this is a reference to the three *Seforim* of *Sefer Yetzirah*], which are *Chochma* (חכמה, wisdom), *Bina* (בינה, understanding) and *Daat,* (דעת, knowledge). And within it are seventy-two names, and this is the secret of Y (י') YH (י"ה) YHV (יה"ו) *YHVH* (יהו"ה) [= 72]; and know and understand this deeply. It is one in the three worlds, and it is in reality one. And its secret is also that it is the '*Keter Torah*' (כתר תורה, crown of the Torah), which is 'twenty six' in its *Cheshbon* [יהו"ה = 26]. And about it *Chazal* said that it stands waiting, and anyone who wants can come and take [from it]; and with [an extra value of one for] the word it contains the 27 letters [i.e. it equals 27], and with it the *Kohen Gadol* (כהן גדול, High Priest) would bless Israel. And its secret is "**As such you shall bless**" (Numbers 6:23), written *Ko Tevarchu* with *Vav* (ו') [=and] (כו תברכו) *Koh Tevarchu*, [and] with *Heh* (ה') (כה תברכו), for the blessing depends on ה"ו; and that is the secret that it indicates; know it! Such is (כה) the whole of the *Shem Meforash* in the number of *Koh Tevarchu*. *Koh* (כ"ה = 25) in the *Shem Meforash*, and *Koh* in the holy language.

Next I will point out to you the pronounced name that is
ADNY (אדני); and its secret in itself is A (א') AD (א"ד)
ADN (אד"נ) ADNY (אדנ"י) [= 126], about which it is said,
"**Established** [*Nachon*, נכו"ן = 126] **was Your throne long
ago**" (Psalms, 93:2). And know that this is a great secret, of
the highest secrets in all *Kabbalah*; and you have to
combine the two together, one after the other, and make a
new word from them in the following fashion: A (א') AD
(א"ד) ADN (אד"נ) ADNY (אדנ"י) ADNYY (אדני"י)
ADNYYH (אדניי"ה) ADNYYHV (אדנייה"ו) ADNY *YHVH*
(אדנייהו"ה), and its secret is "**and in front of My Name he
stood in awe**" (Malachi 2:5). And give it also the opposite
Zeiruf (combination): Y (י') YH (י"ה) YHV (יה"ו) *YHVH*
(יהוה"ד) *YHVH*AD (יהוה"א) *YHVH*A (יהו"ה)
*YHVH*ADN (יהוהאד"נ) *YHVH*ADNY (יהוהאדנ"י). And its
secret is, "*YHVH* **says to my Lord** (אדני): **Sit at My right
hand**" (Psalms, 110:1).

Give praise and thanks to God that I have revealed this
sublime secret of the two names to you, which contains
seventy-two letters. And if you mention them at the right
point in order to sanctify them, you will transform nature
with their coming for sure. And they are each composed of
4 words; and if you add that to their letters, which are 72,
they will combine to [form] *Eved* (עב"ד, slave, servant, a
title of *Metatron*). And these are all divine, transforming
nature, which is the Throne; and that is the secret of, "**This
is the finger of God** (*Elohim*, אלהים)" (Exodus 15:8),
meaning that the finger transforms nature with the power
of the mentioned name, *Elohim*, which is the *Mida*
(attribute) of *Din*.

And I truly know that whenever I or another interpreter
who knows some *Kabbalah* mentions one thing or another

about the transformation of nature, enforced by the power of the knowledge of names, our words will sound very strange and pretty much mistaken to those who inquire after wisdom with their intellects. And these are the philosophers who deem Aristotle to be far greater than the greatest of the prophets, Moses our Rav, may he rest in peace. And I concur with their words of truth, and admit that Aristotle was extremely wise in his enquiries and contemplations, according to what is found in the books of other philosophers and his own books, which testify to his great wisdom. However, he truly never reached the level of those who speak with *Ruach Ha-Kodesh*, which forces those who reach it to speak of their own accords about the [various] levels of reality. And though every man has the potential of *Ruach Ha-Kodesh*, he never realized it, for if he had, he would not have believed the world to be eternal; nevertheless, he never achieved the level of prophesy. And if he had spoken out of the best of his ability, he would have verified for himself and known all the forces that realize the effect that truly transforms nature, as we found among some special prophets who did so according to time and place in order to sanctify God's name, not to go crazy about things of no value such as the gullible crave. And there is evidence for that among the sayings of *Chazal*, meaning that it is possible to transform nature with the power of the knowledge of a name; and that is the saying, "and he who uses a *Taga* (תגא, a crown of the letters) is gone" (*Avot* 4:5). Some interpret *Taga* to be the student of the *Torah*, and he cannot be used. However, its true interpretation is the *Keter Torah*, and they wanted to say that he who uses the *Shem Meforash* transgresses the will of God, for He did not let His name be known to Man except to sanctify Him.

And I already informed you that the unified name is the mysteries of the *Torah*. And if they are not effective, how will they be used? However, for the glory of God it is allowed according to time and place, as the true prophets did, may peace be with them. And as it is written, "**that My Name might be proclaimed in all the earth**" (Exodus 9:16), through the transformation of nature. For the excellence of His name will not be evident to the masses except through that. And thus, when a man says or writes in a book that nature can be transformed, it is wrong of the *Maskil* to falsify him, if he is versed in *Torah*, and considered among its believers. Rather, he shall believe that this can be done by anyone who knows his way about the power of the name. And if he puts his mind to it (Yechaven, יכון, [could also mean perform *Kabbalistic Kavanot* – כוונות, mystical intentions]) he will know the truth about it and will rise from the level of belief to the level of knowledge of it. Nonetheless, there is a sublime secret here that should be concealed even from the *Maskilim*. I cannot but indicate it to you a little, as is necessary at this place. And every *Maskil* knows the issue with the Splitting of the Red Sea as we received it, which is a supreme miracle, as it is known; and that is the issue of the 12 paths for 12 tribes, and it was perceived through and through. And as it was verified with clear cutting proofs by the scientists, among the 3 forms of conception that are called the physical, the imaginary, and the intellectual, the superior one is the intellectual, next is the physical, and next is the imaginary. For the physical is the outwardly perceived, the imaginary is the inwardly perceived, and the intellectual is internal to the inward, and so it is also the secret of the internal inside the internal. Therefore, we today who understand something in that wonder with the power of the knowledge of the name, which is undoubtedly the essence of the issue, we have a clearer concept of it than those who passed through the sea on dry land [and] got through with their physical perception alone. However, there were people there who understood the truth with their intellect, with the power of the knowledge of the name, and they understood it completely, both perceptually and intellectually; they are undoubtedly superior to those who understand it in their mind alone. And so our Rabbis of blessed memory notified us when they called that generation the Knowledgeable Generation, for the least of their women understood wonderful concepts, as they said: "A maid saw on the Sea what Ezekiel the prophet of blessed memory never saw" (*Yalkut Shimoni, Shmot*, Ch. 15). Contemplate what I have told you with a sound intellect, and you shall find the truth concealed therein, for I am not allowed to expand on it any further.

And know that the names that are not erased are 10, and they are: *YHVH* (יהוה), *Adonai* (אדני), *Eloha* (אלוה), El (אל), *Elohim* (אלהים), *Shadai* (שדי), *Tzevaot* (צבאות) [*Eheieh* (אהיה), Yah (יה), *El Chai* (אל חי)]. And these are the names of the blessed Creator, even though they are all descriptions and epithets, except for the first; and we have received that it is forbidden to erase them. And these are the names of the 10 separate [intellects] according to their level: *Chayot Ha-Kodesh* (חיות הקדש), *Ophanim* (אופנים), *Ar'elim* (אראלים), *Chashmalim* (חשמלים), *Seraphim* (שרפים), *Malachim* (מלאכים), *Elim* (אלים), *Bnei Elim* (בני אלים), *Chruvim* (כרובים), *Ishim* (אישים). And so the Rav mentions them in *Sefer Ha-Mada* (ספר המדע), and according to their effects they are different in name. For example, Rephael (רפאל) is responsible for medicine (רפואה, *Refuah*), Gabriel over *Gvurah*, and Samael (סמאל) over the northern [common euphemism for evil]. And so, the place where most of them are derived from is understood immediately. And some cannot be understood unless by *Tzeiruf* of the letters and *Gematria*, like *Shadai*, which is Metatron in *Gematria*, or *Par* (פר, bull), which is Sandalfon (סנדלפון) in *Gematria*. And similarly are many that contain wonderful secrets in their *Tzeiruf*. For example, Sandalfon becomes "in the burning bush he drew up my face" (בסנה דלה פני); and Metatron becomes *Mentator* (מנטטור), that is Guardian; and that is the secret of [the name] *Shadai*, which is written on the *Mezuzah* on the outside, meaning that it is the keeper of the house and its guardian. And it is the keeper of the gate at the end of the secret of the ten *Maamarot* (מאמרות, utterances) in which the world was created; he removes the *Yetzer Ha-Ra* in the secret of *Mezuza"h* [=65], and that is the pronounced name Adonai [=65], which together with Shadai is lentil (עדש"ה = 379 = 314+65) in *Gematria*. And a demon will not be created in [something] smaller than a lentil. And know that this is an extremely great secret if you shall know it [and conceal it] in the chamber of your heart.

And I already told you what could be revealed about the *Shem Meforash* and the pronounced name. And you already know that the name *El* is derived from power, as it is written, "It is within my hand (לאל ידי, *Le-El Yadi*)" (Genesis 31:29), meaning "the power is in my hand". *Eheieh*, however, refers to eternal existence — meaning, "I will be (אהיה) forever". And the evidence is, "I will be that I will be" (Exodus, 3:14), which is "I will be" without change "that I will be" for all [lit. without] eternity. And so did the Rav say in the *Guide* that it refers to the necessary existence and the eternity. And so also for *Shadai*, meaning that His essence is sufficient for all created beings, i.e., that

He is enough (ד'י, *Dai*). And about *Tzevaot Chazal* said that He is a sign (אות, *Ot*) amongst His hosts (צבא, *Tzava*). And understand that they were talking about *Tzeiruf*, for they divided [the word] *Tzevaot* into two and added to it so as to complete [lit. "not to complete"] the intention behind the *Tzeiruf*, even though it contains no trace of it. And beyond these, there are others that should be concealed from the public, but the *Mitzva* is in handing them down verbally after due supplements. And of the above mentioned separate names the first are **Chayot Ha-Kodesh**, and this name is derived from "vitality" (חיות, *Chayut*) and "holiness", referring to the most excellent living beings and the closest to the origin of holiness. And the Rav said they are all cause and effect, the one existing due to the power of the other; and they are superior to all that is among the created beings. However, *Chayot Ha-Kodesh* are also among those who receive the *Shefa* of the most supreme beginning of all reality. For we have received that the beings were not created, even though prior to the creation of the world there was nothing along with the blessed Creator except for Him and His name alone.

Know this considerable matter, and contemplate it with a sound intellect following the *Kabbalah*. And this is all so that you do not fail [to understand] the beings, for the secret of creation is not understood immediately by every *Maskil*. Indeed, knowing the secret of creation you will know the very essence of *Maase Bereshit* (מעשה בראשית, Act of Genesis), even though what we are talking about is none other than *Maase Merkava* (מעשה מרכבה, the Act of *Merkava*). And study what *Chazal* has instructed us about the words *Maase Merkava* and *Maase Bereshit*. And *Maase Merkava* and *Maase Bereshit* are allegorically like male and female.

Ophanim (אופנים), indicates that they are a *Tzeiruf* of *Chayot Ha-Kodesh*, for this name is derived from the singular *Ophan* (אופן, wheel), except that they are many, and it is also derived from the *Tzeiruf* of the internality (הפנימיות).

Ar'elim (אראלים), means *Ar'e Elim* (אראה אלים, I will see powers), and they are visible below by the power of the *Ophanim*.

Chashmalim (חשמלים): *Chazal* said that sometimes they are *Chashot* (חשות, anxious) and sometimes *Memalelot* (ממללות, speaking), i.e., sometimes silent sometimes speaking. And know that this is a sublime secret, as Ezekiel the prophet said of the *Chashmal* that it is above the *Rakia* (רקיע, firmament).

Seraphim (שרפים) is derived from burning (שריפה, *Srepha*), for they burn anybody who gets too close.

Malachim (מלאכים) means messengers, for any assigned messenger is called a Malach (מלאך, messenger, angel).

Elim (אלים), Bnei Elim (בני אלים): I already told you that this name is derived from power, though the power of the father is not as the power of the son, for it never changes.

Chruvim (כרובים) is the young ones, for a child is called *Chruvia* (כרוביא). And there are two *Chruvim* in Man, who speak to him one from this side and one from the other, and [he is] the decider among them. As it is said, "He placed in front of the Garden of Eden *Chruvim* and a flaming sword flashing back and forth to guard the path to the tree of life" (Genesis 3:24). From between the whispering *Chruvim* the flaming of the flashing sword is like lightning guarding the *Torah* and the wisdom, which is the path to the Tree of Life like a garden planted in Eden; and understand!

Ishim (אישים) is the one called the Active Intellect; and because this degree is divided among the personalities (*Ishim*) of human beings, they are called by their name by analogy. And not that they are individual personalities, for their level is of general unity. And this is the last level among the separate intellects, and it sheds its influence upon us by the life that is above it, in order to bring back the *Nefesh* of Man to its eternity; and the existence of the one is the existence of the other. And it is with the First, [in] the secret of "**Every tenth will be holy to God**" (Leviticus 27:32). And after I mentioned to you the names of the *Malachim* in general, I will let you know the names of the inferior ones in general according to their kind, as far as my abilities go, with the help of God.

And know that the name "sphere" applies to everything that is ball shaped and round, for the spheres are like balls, front and back in fire and in water – a *Malach*. And it is said that it is male and female; such peace will be peace. From here on it is missing in the copy, and may God find us worthy to find it and copy it. Hence, I left two vacant pages here (comment by the copyist).

...and truly, when the *Nefesh* separates from the body, its level is far superior to the material spheres, and it is concealed under the Throne of Glory, which is above it. And I already informed you of the secret of *Sar Tzevaot* above, by the way of *Kabbalah*. And he said of the seventh, that is **Adonai**, which is derived from pardon and mercy, and I think this is because it indicated lordship (אדנות, *Adnut*); and a good lord is merciful to his servants. However, I already let you know my opinion – that it indicates the righteous – and it is known that the righteous is someone who has received *Shefa* from righteousness (צדקה, *Tzdaka*, also charity), as I told you that the unified [name] indicates righteousness in the secret of the great world; and so it is called the righteous as a description, for it is also constantly drawn to it. And I informed you of other things about it too. And I will say of the eighth, which is the unified [name], what *Chazal* have interpreted about it: as it is said, "priests on the Day of Atonement". It is the one that is not heard except in the Temple, and even when the *Kohen Gadol* began to utter it, everyone would answer *Beshekmal"o* in a loud voice, so that they did not hear the literal [utterance] mentioned 10 times at the Day of Atonement in the Temple. And why is the occasion so special? And why on that special day? And why 10 times? And why in the Temple, and why by the *Kohen Gadol*? All these contain sublime matters and superior holy secrets by the way of *Kabbalah*. And I mentioned all I can.

He said of the ninth, that it is holy, and it is the secret of the hearer [of the words that come] from the mouths of *Seraphim* and *Chruvim*, as it is written, "**And they were calling to one another**" (Isaiah 6:3). Nevertheless, we do not have it from *Chazal* that it is neither to be erased, nor the next one that is the tenth, which is king. They called them "epithets", and so they are like the other holy letters and it is allowed to erase them. And they are similar to compassionate, merciful, righteous, and such like, that are descriptions and epithets derived from the effects. And the secret that we received and consider holy is, as has been said in *Sefer Yetzira*, "in 231 (רל"א, *Ral"a*) gates"; and its sign is *Aleph* (א'), *Mem* ('מ), *Shin* ('ש), and on the other hand its sign is *Rae"l* (רא"ל [of Israel] = 231); and it relies on the alphabet, and its secret is the additional *Chayot Ha-Kodesh* above everything; and they are the beginning, and their sign is *Bereshit* (בראשית, in the beginning). Do not read it *Bereshit*, but "[He] created six" (*Bara Shit*, ברא שית); and in *Tzeiruf* it becomes "at the head is *T[h]ei*" (בראש תי), which in Greek means God, with an interdental "T" and the vowel "ei". And its secret is different than any other language, for all the languages are included, as languages, in *Lashon Ha-Kodesh* (לשון הקודש, the holy language), which is built of 22 letters and five vowels, as I will discuss below with God's help; for there can be no speech and no script without it, and there can be no change in the letters that are holy, as it is *Lashon Ha-Kodesh, Ko"f* (קו"ף), *Dale"t* (דל"ת), *Va"v* (וי"ו), *Shi"n* (שי"ן). And He is *Tei* in Greek *Tav* (תי"ו), *Yud* (יו"ד), and He is called *Shento* [?] (שנתו) in a foreign language, *Shin* (שי"ן), *Nun* (נו"ן), *Tav* (תי"ו), *Vav* (וי"ו), or *Tet* (טי"ת), *Vav* (וי"ו). And similarly, if you mention Him in 70 languages, the letters will always be those of *Lashon Ha-Kodesh*, and it is all the same, except that that language is prepared for those who know, and not prepared for those who do not know His name; hence, this is a sublime issue, for it contains a great secret. And it is known from the verse, "**Now the whole earth had one language and a common speech**" (Genesis 11:1), and after that in general, including the languages of the whole earth. And it is also known from a verse that is said about the Messiah: "**Then will I purify the lips of the peoples, that all of them may call on the name of God and serve Him shoulder to shoulder**" (Zefania 3:9); and everyone [will] know that the seventy languages are included in *Lashon Ha-Kodesh* as we have said.

He said of the tenth – which is king – that it points to the issue of His existence as the King of Kings. And after I mentioned to you the interpretation of the 10 names as the

Gaon of blessed memory spoke about them, I will mention the name of 12, the name of 14, the name of 42, the name of 72, and then names of the *Malachim* who serve before Him, as did the Rav in the *Guide*. And they are ten according to their levels – external, intermediary, and internal – and they are: *Chayot Ha-Kodesh* (חיות הקדש), *Ophanim* (אופנים), *Ar'elim* (אראלים), *Chashmalim* (חשמלים), *Seraphim* (שרפים), *Malachim* (מלאכים), *Elim* (אלים), *Bnei Elim* (בני אלים), *Cruvim* (כרובים), and *Ishim* (אישים). And you already know that these names are plural, in order to indicate that no one of them is unified in its unity like its Creator, but they are all compound, even though they also drive and control what is below them. And the Rav of blessed memory said that *Chayot Ha-Kodesh* is a derived name from "vitality" and "holiness". And so it seems they are all derived according to their effects; and sometimes they are called by a name that literally indicates the effect, such as Rephael over medicine, Gabriel over *Gvurah* and over sex, from the root of *Gavra* (גברא, manhood), and Samael over the northern, i.e. the *Yetzer Ha-Ra*. And thus, where most of them come from and what their effects are is immediately understood by their names. And sometimes they are named due to *Gematrias* and acronyms, or by the *Tzeiruf* of the letters, such as *Shadai* (שדי) that is Metatron (מטטרון) in *Gematria*, *Par* (פ"ר) - [that is] Sandalfon (סנדלפון) in *Gematria*, and one is *Rochev* (רוכב, driving), and the other is *Murkav* (מורכב, lit. being driven, also compound) [both words related to the *Merkava*]. And know this, for it is a great secret. And there are many others like this, such as Sandalfon in "at Sinai he drew up my face", Metatron [who] is the Guardian, *Chashmal Chashot Memalelot*, which is the secret of [the mountains] Grizim and Eival, and it is an acronym of *Chochma* (חכמה, wisdom) *Shalom* (שלום, peace) *Malchut Levush* (לבוש, garment), and so on, also *Tzeiruf* such as *Tzevaot* [with] "He is a sign amongst His hosts", and so forth.

And the sayings of *Chazal* should enlighten you plenty on all the words of *Kabbalah*. And contemplate everything that I mentioned, and everything that I did not mention, for it all converges on the same place. And also, be enlightened by the components of the words: even if they are not nouns or descriptions, they contain wonderful secrets. And be enlightened also by the names of the figures appearing in the *Torah*, for concerning many of them, what they are in their essence is explicitly written, such as Adam (אדם) from "soil" (אדמה), Eve (חוה) "the mother of all living" (אם כל חי), Cain (קין) from "acquired" (קניתי), Shet (שת) from "**God has appointed me another seed**" (שת לי אלהים זרע) (Genesis 4:25), Noah (נח) "will comfort us" (ינחמנו), Abraham (אברהם) is "the father of many" (אב המון), Itzchak (יצחק) from "laughter" (מצחוק), Jacob (יעקב) from "footstep" (עקב), Esav (עשו) "is made" (עשוי), Edom (אדם) "over redness" (על האדום), Reuven (ראובן) "has seen" (ראה), Shimon (שמעון) "has heard" (שמע), Levi (לוי) "will lend" (ילוה), Yehuda (יהודה) "I give thanks" (אודה), Isachar (יששכר) "my reward" (שכרי), Zevulun (זבולון) "will nourish me" (יזבליני), Dan (דן) "will judge me" (דנני), Naphtali (נפתלי) is "my twisting and turning" (נפתולי), Gad (גד) "fortune comes" (בא גד), Asher (אשר) "I have been affirmed" (אישרוני), Yoseph (יוסף) "has gathered" (אסף), Benyamin (בנימין) "the son of my strength" (בן אוני), Moshe (משה) "I have pulled him out" (משיתיהו), Gershom (גרשם) "is stranger" (גר), Eliezer (אליעזר) is "in my aid" (בעזרי) [they are all

Hebrew puns]. And contemplate these, for they are all full of gems containing precious secrets. And these are the words of *Kabbalah*. And all the reasons of *Torah* are contained in *Kabbalah* for the knowledge of truth about the world, and for no other purpose, as according to the opinions of those who write names for hatred and love, and similar types of madness that carry no smell and no flavor. And I have already mentioned to you the truth about the whole of the perceptual and intellectual reality, and the internal and external nature of mankind, and the revealed and concealed paths of prophecy, which depend on the letters, the words, and the *Cheshbon*; and I discussed their qualities from every side. And the *Torah* is the middle, the Tree of Life, as it is written, "In the middle of the garden were the tree of life and the tree of the knowledge of good and evil" (Genesis 2:9).

And now I will enlighten you generally by way of conclusion. And know that there are 3 ('ג) types of *Nefesh* among the inferior ones. And the types of *Nefesh* of the superior ones are 9 ('ט), so that all those who have a *Nefesh* in general are *Ge"t* (ג"ט, 12). And the superior ones belong to the spheres — from the sphere of the moon to the circumspective sphere — and the inferior ones are the vegetative, the perceiving, and the speaking. And you already know that everything is made for the sake of something else, such as the vegetative *Nefesh* of Man, which exists prior to the perceiving *Nefesh* for the sake of the perceiving *Nefesh*. And [so] the perceiving *Nefesh*, which is prior to the speaking *Nefesh*; and the speaking *Nefesh* also exists for the sake of something else, and that is the intellect (for the lower is created for the sake of the higher). And in it are found the 9 types of *Nefesh* in general in the spheres, in order to understand the intellect with them, as the intellect is found among created beings in order to understand the Creator with it. And so the perfect *Maskil* should shed off the 3 above mentioned types of *Nefesh* to the best of his ability and be clothed in his intellectual form found along with him, in order to be perfected by the understanding of the blessed Creator and the created beings, as far as he can. And [he should] not be burdened by more than he can take, for every excess is like having none; for he knows that the form of the *Nefesh* is the intellect, as the form of the body is the *Nefesh*. And similarly, all the letters are embodiments, and the dots are like the *Nefesh* in them, which are the five vowels *Kamatz* (קמץ, long 'a'), *Tzeire* (צירה, long 'e'), *Cholam* (חולם, 'o'), *Chirik* (חיריק 'i'), and *Shuruk* (שורוק, 'u'). And their sign is *Notareikun* (נוֹטָרְיְקוֹן, acronym), or *Ligvuloteah* (לגבולותיה, to her borders) [both words contain all five vowels]. And the sign of their *Cheshbon* is "the end of wonders" in this image: A (אָ), I (אִ), O (אֹ), U (אוּ), E (אֶ). And there is no speech without them, and no articulation uses more than them. And they contain 3 worlds: upper, middle, and lower. And similarly, speech is divided into three: voice, wind, and speech. And so did *Chazal* say, "a dot in the letters of the *Torah* resembles the *Neshama* among men"; and they said in *Yerushalmi* , "a dot of *Torah* in the word resembles among letters the *Neshama* in the body of a man", meaning that the vowels among the letters are like the *Neshamah* among men. And consider that they said "as the *Neshamot* in the body", which are not the final purpose but what comes after them.

And that is understanding, which they consider to be in the intellect along with the *Nefesh*, so that there is no benefit, truth, and perfection in the body and in the *Nefesh* without the existence of the intellect, just as there is no benefit, truth, and perfection in the letters and the vowels without understanding their meaning. And it is known that if the *Nefesh* does not assume the form of the intellect, it is not perfect before [or together with] its blessed Creator. And its existence is not good with no knowledge, as it is written, "**Also, without knowledge, the *Nefesh* is not good**" (Proverbs: 19:2); and the opposite case – i.e., when the intellect exists in the *Nefesh* while it is still in the body – is said, "**Better to me is the *Torah* from your mouth than thousands of pieces of silver and gold**" (Psalms, 119:72) [the previous verse begins with a *Gimmel* ('ג), and this one with a *Tet* ('ט). Together they spell out *Get* (גט)], meaning that I become better with the existence of the *Torah* given by Your mouth – that is the intellect – than with the most excellent body and *Nefesh*. And he symbolised the *Nefesh* with gold, and the body with silver. And know that all this is a demonstration of what I informed you about [discussing] names without knowing their qualities. And I showed you for example what my intention was in calling this book *Get*, due to the quality of removing all things for which the purpose intended for them is not known. And consider what I said, that the purpose demanded of Man is to understand from the words of the prophet what is hidden and concealed in the qualities of the word components and names, until through them the final end of understanding is reached on all sides, which is the knowledge of the name [of God]; and loving it; and fearing it. And God, for the sake of His name, will find us worthy to understand the secrets of His perfect *Torah* and its mysteries, so that we will find *Chen* (חן, grace) in His eyes through the knowledge of His name and its paths. As it is written, "**May You show me Your ways, that I may know You, and that I may find *Chen* in Your sight**" (Exodus 33:13).